The Summer of Madness

by

Alexander Raphael

To mum, dad and sis

It was the summer of love. Or the summer of madness. The weather was glorious. Sunshine all through the day, picnics and barbecues and sandals and bees everywhere. Cafes and pubs with outdoor gardens were making a killing and huge numbers of people were taking advantage and heading right to the beach. There seemed a reduction in crime, reported at least, and an increase in feel-good stories. In glorious sunshine that covered every shade of yellow, why get angry?

Wedding numbers were up, the value of them too, so every kind of business seemed to be benefitting. Every day seemed to produce a new study highlighting the modern trend of romance. More people were finding greater success on dating websites, couples in love were living longer than single people, romantic getaways were more common than ever. And for everyone. People over 70 were finally finding love again more often than ever before, showing it was never too late.

Several A-listers were finally tying the knot or getting together, including a proud lifelong bachelor. A much-loved TV presenter had finally been able to conceive after years of trying. There were two royal weddings. One destined not to last, one lasting when it would have been better not to. The times for explosive rumours of cheating with the nanny, co-stars and impressionable fans and any number of speculative behaviours were years away.

Everywhere was romance. And ordinary people's lives seemed more interesting than ever. There was a story about a woman who'd never had a boyfriend or any physical affection finally finding her Prince Charming after an internet campaign. Video blogs were posted throughout her search, gathering momentum all the way. Her joy was a victory for everyone. Rumours of a film or TV show were flying around.

Another story was of a woman who, diagnosed as having cancer, decided she would be grateful for what life had given her. The 42-year-old solicitor decided to track down and thank the people who had most had an impact on her life. What started off as a touching story became romantic when she fell head over heels for the son of a nurse who had helped take care of her when she had a near deadly bout of flu. And as if that wasn't enough of a happy story, treatment had been going well and her cancer was now in remission.

But no, those weren't the only stories out there that summer those years back. One other stood out.

It all started simply enough. After two years together, a woman realised that her boyfriend seemed to enjoy spending time more with his video games and friends than with her. She'd had enough and was done. She even left the break up note on his gaming console. "I warned you. Enjoy your gaming. Don't contact me again."

Though she had warned him numerous times before, he had never taken it seriously. His high scores and his football and drinks with the guys had seemed so important. Now it all seemed so worthless. And telling himself that he could close the door and get her back even after she'd bolted, he set to work. He sent her long heartfelt texts. He left voicemails. He rang her at her office and even serenaded her at her apartment. The flowers and chocolates got no love either.

Then he switched to her friends. He begged and pleaded for them to put a good word in. After strong orders from the girl and threats of severe repercussions if they broke rank, his desperation fell on deaf ears. Again and again.

So he stepped it up. He got her front-row tickets to see her favourite band, got her a VIP invite at a very exclusive music festival and even managed to convince a well-known TV star to leave her a personalised voicemail. All to no avail. And all very expensive. And the celebrity wasn't happy either, later claiming he'd been lied to and that he'd been told the girl had been ill.

None of it was working. And he was running out of ideas. And that's where most people would have given up, if not far, far, sooner. But our man was nothing if not persistent. And so he decided to go for it, with one last idea. Something romantic but dramatic, poetic but effective. And that's probably where he got the idea from.

"1801.— I have just returned from a visit to my landlord—the solitary neighbour that I shall be troubled with."

People didn't know what to think when the previously rugged but now clean-cut 30-year-old in a well-pressed suit started reading from his chair outside the town's busy train station early one Monday morning. People shot him funny glances as they walked past him, wondering who this weird eccentric was. Some carried on walking, while others decided to linger a few moments longer, wondering if they could make sense of it.

"This is certainly a beautiful country! In all England, I do not believe that I could have fixed on a situation so completely removed from the stir of society."

He read at a slow pace, which was probably just as well. It was an old text, though of course a famous one. People who knew the classic well would know, but a few more smiled and nodded when an iconic character got his first mention.

"A perfect misanthropist's heaven: and Mr. Heathcliff and I are such a suitable pair to divide the desolation between us."

That seemed to be the moment most people who had been listening, or at least paying some form of attention, noticed the sign next to him.

"My name is Kurt. I was an idiot. I took my girlfriend for granted. I will read her favourite book *Wuthering Heights* to you every day until I win her back."

And Kurt continued to read. *"He little imagined how my heart warmed towards him when I beheld his black eyes withdraw so suspiciously under their brows, as I rode up, and when his fingers sheltered themselves, with a jealous resolution, still further in his waistcoat, as I announced my name."*

Anyone there would have smiled at some of the more humorous observations made by people as they became fully aware of the situation.

"That's a short note for a long book, must be saving his energy" was one. "Wow, his girlfriend really did throw the book at him" was another. "What a novel idea" got the biggest response.

An unintentional laugh came when someone remarked that Jane Austen would be rolling in her grave. When a guy commented if the Bronte woman's other books would get bigger sales now, his girlfriend just smiled without feeling the need to make any corrections.

As people started getting to work, the crowds did die down, but there was still a number of loyal and curious people who refused to move. That included some, concentrating on the story, and others, focused more on him. This wasn't a city where there were entertainers. There were no jugglers, dancers, singers or musicians. Not even protesters. This was a quiet town unused to any form of attention grabbing. And here was this stranger making a fool of himself, or making himself worthy. People couldn't really seem to decide. But they were watching.

And as people came out for lunch, the numbers rose back up. Those who were already comfortable watching him found themselves bumped and nudged as new people wanted to edge closer. Some were people who had missed him first time around. Some were those wanting to know if he was still there. And more still who had heard smatterings of news of some "crazy dude who messed up big time" and were curious to know more.

By this stage, Kurt was on the early stages of Chapter 4.

"Oh, I'll turn the talk on my landlord's family!' I thought to myself. 'A good subject to start! And that pretty girl-widow, I should like to know her history: whether she be a native of the country, or, as is more probable, an exotic that the surly indigenae will not recognise for kin.' With this intention I asked Mrs. Dean why Heathcliff let Thrushcross Grange, and preferred living in a situation and residence so much inferior. 'Is he not rich enough to keep the estate in good order?' I inquired."

He took a sip of water and continued.

"Rich, sir!' she returned. 'He has nobody knows what money, and every year it increases. Yes, yes, he's rich enough to live in a finer house than this: but he's very near—close-handed; and, if he had meant to flit to Thrushcross Grange, as soon as he heard of a good tenant he could not have borne to miss the chance of getting a few hundreds more. It is strange people should be so greedy, when they are alone in the world!

Kurt carried on reading, but onlookers were getting impatient and wanted to know more. "Do you really think this will work?", "Won't your voice get hoarse?", "Did you cheat on her?" "Is she really worth all this?" What hours will you read until?"

The guy paused after each one, considered them, then carried on reading. When a young local guy went to ask more, he got shushed, with his error explained by the crowd's most devoted listener: "I like this bit. It's when the housekeeper starts to explain to Lockwood more about Heathcliff and Catherine, having just stayed in the haunted room."

"Haunted room?"

"Yes, where Lockwood saw the ghost of Catherine who's desperate to be let in"

"Who's Catherine?"

"She's the great love of Heathcliff. She and him had this intense... Oh blast, you're making me miss it." With that she scowled and turned back to face the narrator.

She was so fierce that everyone quietened down as Kurt carried on. *"Why, sir, she is my late master's daughter: Catherine Linton was her maiden name. I nursed her, poor thing! I did wish Mr. Heathcliff would remove here, and then we might have been together again."*

Those who were on lunch breaks and indeed had finished eating, knew they would have to get going soon. That didn't include the girl from earlier who, though uncomfortable standing, was not going anywhere. Kurt straightened his tie and continued.

"What! Catherine Linton?' I exclaimed, astonished. But a minute's reflection convinced me it was not my ghostly Catherine. Then,' I continued, 'my predecessor's name was Linton?'
'It was.'
'And who is that Earnshaw: Hareton Earnshaw, who lives with Mr. Heathcliff? Are they relations?'
'No; he is the late Mrs. Linton's nephew"

The guy from earlier repeatedly tapped on the girl's shoulder, later identified as Judy, who just said "Fine, fine, I'll explain later".

And so, everyone carried on for another hour until the narrator quietly finished Chapter 5. As he walked off, there was still a fairly strong number. Some had come and gone and a few had even returned, but the girl from earlier was still there, using a newspaper as a makeshift blanket to sit on. She was too shy to say anything.

Whether they admitted it to themselves, the next day there was an increase in people going in early to work. And maybe they wondered if he would still be there. He wouldn't be the first to make a commitment and then back out when it got inconvenient.

But there he was, again in a suit, though this time in a more subtle grey one. The more observant in the crowd would have noticed a few additions to his reading area. Namely, a few small placards, placed upright on the ground. One said simply: "Yes she is worth it." A second one, next to it said: "No, I did not cheat" and a final one merely "8.30am – 12.30pm"

Judy, the blonde 21-year-old student who had made a lot more effort with her appearance, was at the front. She had brought along her well-thumbed copy of *Wuthering Heights*, a neatly prepared packed lunch and a portable chair and blanket. She wasn't going anywhere.

Behind her a few people filmed him but weren't really sure what to do with their footage. When to start filming and when to finish? What exactly were they really filming on their phones? Who would react to it?

Undistracted by the world around him, Kurt began Chapter 6.

"Mr. Hindley came home to the funeral; and—a thing that amazed us, and set the neighbours gossiping

right and left—he brought a wife with him. What she was, and where she was born, he never informed us: probably, she had neither money nor name to recommend her, or he would scarcely have kept the union from his father."

And though the background chatter inconveniently rose at certain levels, and photos were shot and certain parts filmed, he carried on. Questions answered by the placards were pointed out, as well as new questions posed, but nothing was going to distract him. He simply waited until it was quiet again and carried on with the story.

His was a rather ordinary voice. He made no effort to give different characters an accent, and his attempts at getting Joseph the Yorkshire caretaker were gamely but comical. But it was largely a sympathetic audience. Those unamused or uninterested would shout out passing unpleasantries but were quickly hounded out.

He took careful sips but otherwise read at a steady pace. Some followed his text on their phone or their own copy and would correct if he missed a line while others were happy just to listen.

But while he was focusing on the story, word was getting around in the town still further. Whether through the photos and videos being posted online, or by more traditional forms of gossip, more people were hearing about it. And more influential ones too.

When Kurt came to read his story again the next morning, there were surprises for Judy and a mix of loyal followers and passers-by. He put down an extra placard that had raised a slight gasp as it had a photo of the woman in question. Though it was mostly in silhouette and she had sunglasses on, she was certainly striking. A Mediterranean beauty with dark hair that cascaded past her shoulders. Judy scowled silently, while others were happy to use words ranging from "Fair dos" to "What an idiot!"

But there was also a surprise for him. There was a reporter from the local newspaper ready with a list of questions. He introduced himself politely enough and his enthusiasm for the interview seemed genuine and heartfelt. It wasn't. But though he was relatively new to the journalism industry, the 27-year-old journalist knew most people either couldn't tell fake sincerity or else didn't care.

Not this time though. The narrator said: "I'll answer some questions after I've finished. But I need to get on with the story."

'Cathy, are you busy this afternoon?' asked Heathcliff.
'Are you going anywhere?'
'No, it is raining,' she answered.

'Why have you that silk frock on, then?' he said. 'Nobody coming here, I hope?'
'Not that I know of,' stammered Miss: 'but you should be in the field now, Heathcliff. It is an hour past dinnertime: I thought you were gone.'

The journalist tried talking over him but knew he was fighting a losing battle. Not only with the narrator, but with others wanting to listen to more of the story. That didn't include a quiet Judy, who failed to notice that Marcus, the guy from yesterday had bought a copy of the book, along with a notepad and a very basic description of the characters. When he had later asked her to check it, she gave a half glance but continued on listening. A slight frown passed as he pondered her reaction, and her focus on the book.

The journalist instead sent off a quick email and then started drafting his article. Though he was more interested in politics and harder hitting news reporting, he knew the game. He wouldn't be trusted to interview government ministers and CEOs until he proved himself with the more maverick and novelty stories. It might even be his big break if he could get the right quotes. He started fine tuning his questions.

Amusingly, when describing the "tall, well-groomed and sensitive-looking 30-year-old", the journalist failed to notice there was more than a passing similarity between Kurt and himself. Which was probably just as well. He already had enough to focus on with the novel, audience description and how he was going to structure the article.

Judy was still interested in the story but was evidently both sulking and plotting her next move. Marcus, her admirer, was concentrating on the story, adding to his notes and keeping an eye on Judy. The rest of the audience were blissfully unaware of their struggles.

While this was happening, a hot dog salesman had decided to use a bit of initiative. Unhappy with how far away his hot dog stall was from the action, he got one of his workers to take over while he went out with a large basket of hot dogs and sauces, a menu board and all kinds of change. Not to mention plenty of napkins. Initially there was a slow response, but after one person bought one, numerous others soon followed. He had no idea how long the book was or even what it was about, but he'd take the extra business while he could get it.

And he wasn't the only one. The owner of the town's local bookshop, who drove to work, had noticed that sales of *Wuthering Heights* were up. Not knowing what the reason was as she usually worked in the back part of the store and her staff all lived locally, she nevertheless decided to make a more prominent display in the window. As well as showcasing the different editions they had available, she also set it up to show the works of Emily Bronte's sisters Charlotte and Anne.

It really was wonderfully done and increased sales.

'I'd wrench them off her fingers, if they ever menaced me,' he answered, brutally, when the door had closed after her. 'But what did you mean by teasing the creature in that manner, Cathy? You were not speaking the truth, were you?'

'I assure you I was,' she returned. 'She has been dying for your sake several weeks, and raving about you this morning, and pouring forth a deluge of abuse, because I represented your failings in a plain light, for the purpose of mitigating her adoration. But don't notice it further: I wished to punish her sauciness, that's all. I like her too well, my dear Heathcliff, to let you absolutely seize and devour her up.'

Kurt was nearly at the end of Chapter 10 as the clock struck 12.31. He went to put his book away but Judy, who knew the book so well, coughed politely. Looking at her, then down again at his book, he smiled warmly and then read the last two paragraphs.

The journalist, already impatient, found his patience further tested with the slight delay. If he had been less bothered, he might have noticed Judy more. He had failed to give her a specific reference in his notes and how she had decided that no, she was not going to give up on Kurt. She was going to fight. Clean, dirty, she wasn't giving up on him.

Marcus was also planning on his course of action. Having already read chapter summaries of the book, he spent his time reading a range of provocative and challenging essays, as well as a few silly ones he felt he could impress her with by tearing their arguments to shreds. He wasn't to know that as it stood, his chances were now next to nothing.

As Kurt finally finished with a long glass of water, the journalist elbowed everyone out of the way as he went to get his questions answered. In a quiet voice Kurt explained he was going for lunch but the journalist was welcome to join him and Kurt would be happy to answer once he'd rested his voice. He'd be happy to give the journalist a lift. Unbeknownst to both of them, was that Judy was a skilled lipreader and was able to ascertain where they were going. She set off to buy a broadsheet newspaper as cover and get a taxi to the restaurant.

Marcus, along with anyone else curious to know where they were going, was too slow to act and lost out on all the information. As he put his papers away, he noticed Judy was gone, as was Kurt. He panicked until he ascertained from asking a guy near the front that the "fit blonde who's well out of your league" had hurried to the high street while Kurt had left with a "pretty chatty young-ish guy".

Marcus spent the rest of the day wondering who this guy could be, and why Kurt had decided to leave with him. After all, Kurt didn't seem to like chatting with anyone, not even the gorgeous blonde. What did Kurt have that he didn't? he asked himself.

After going through all kinds of possibilities, he came to the conclusion that this new guy must be a journalist. And as Tafterton was so remote, it surely couldn't be a national paper. It could only be The Tafterton Times. As morning came, he made sure he was there early to grab a paper. Noticing the huge front page mention and reference to a small article in yesterday's paper, he then read the feature three times, each time with a different expression and reaction.

Modern Day Heathcliffe desperate to get back his Cathy

Is romance dead? A 30-year-old data technician is challenging that idea after coming up with a maverick idea to win back his girlfriend through the help of one of literature's most complex love stories.

Kurt Vannes has spent the last two days reading Emily Bronte's powerhouse novel Wuthering Heights outside Tafterton railway station in a drastic effort to get his ex-girlfriend back.

In an exclusive interview with The Tafterton Times, and the first he has given to anyone, the man himself reveals why he is on this romantic odyssey, what his friends and family think of it all and how confident he is of winning her back.

"It's her favourite book. She was always trying to get me to read it"

Anyone passing the heart of Tafterton during the hours of 8.30am and 12.30pm will have noticed a well dressed, impeccably groomed and shy-looking man reading the Yorkshire-set masterpiece. Anyone who was listening to him read the 434 page novel may well have wondered what was going on, especially if they hadn't noticed the small sign he had next to where he was reading.

It was as simple as it was short: My name is Kurt. I was an idiot. I took my girlfriend for granted. I will read her favourite book Wuthering Heights to you every day until I win her back.

Some context is of course necessary. Vannes dated his chef girlfriend (whom he won't name) for two years having met at a café when they were both waiting for friends, who were then both late. After a promising start including romantic trips abroad, she dumped him after tiring of his regular nights of going out drinking with his friends, the constant hours he spent on his wide array of video games and the lack of effort with planning time together.

Despite repeated efforts, and numerous gestures like including getting front row tickets to see her favourite band The Rolling Stones and VIP tickets to popular music festival Bestival, it has all been to no avail. Which brings us to the "nuclear option" as Vannes puts it.

There really are so many questions. First of all, where did the idea for this come from? Has he really considered everything? After all, for a guy who describes himself as "quite introverted for the most part", isn't it all rather mad? Surely his family and friends tried to talk him out of it when he told them?

Still wearing his suit from his earlier reading, Vannes sounds single minded as he looks me in the eyes and answers.

"I told my parents, who understandably were quite concerned," Vannes' says matter-of-factly. Vannes' parents met at school and have been together ever since. Lindsay is a primary school teacher and William is a retired engineer. Kurt is their only child.

"They think I'm going to embarrass myself. They used every argument they could think of. But I'm a romantic just like them. They've been together

for over 40 years and it was love at first sight for both of them. There's nothing they could have said to talk me out of it. I haven't told my friends. And no, I haven't told Fuchsia (the pseudonym Vannes gives for his ex-girlfriend based on her favourite colour) either."

"She actually mentioned it as her favourite book on our first date"

There's a strong argument he should have told her, but then Fuchsia may well not have read it anyway. She hasn't contacted him in any form since the note. Something that hasn't deterred Vannes. The significance of a book about a famously tortured romantic couple isn't lost on him. After all, the free-spirited Cathy and the brooding and intense Heathcliffe aren't the easiest of matches, to say the least!

"She actually mentioned it as her favourite book on our first date", says Vannes, who admits that he hasn't read the 1846 classic, and isn't a huge reader in general, preferring articles on sports and films. "She was always trying to get me to read it and I never did. I did mean to see the film."

When I ask him his thoughts on the book it's clear he struggles with the intense descriptions. "The book is pretty wordy and a bit slow going at the beginning but you can see it start to take shape and I am enjoying it. But there's a reason their love story has resonated. It's not simple but it's still meant to be."

Hmmmm. There are certainly plenty of surprises left for Vannes as he and his followers navigate through. And what has he thought of the response so far? Does he get distracted by the crowd, either fans of the gesture or those that consider him a public menace? After all, rumours are he has generated a loyal set of fans while also being spat at, laughed at and jeered by others.

"At first I noticed it more. On the first day, there was hardly anyone and I probably got through the opening chapter without anyone really paying attention. The few comments that were shouted at I did hear. I think they thought I was trying to sell something or get signatures for a protest or march. And as that's the town's busiest part of the morning, I thought that would be it until lunch. But there seemed to be a few people who stayed around for a bit."

Was the spitting part true?

"Yes, but he didn't get near enough for it to go anywhere near me and his friends dragged him away before he started. Sure, it wasn't pleasant, but it wasn't going to stop me. I've heard the odd shout of "loser", but nothing I pay too much

attention to. And I've noticed the crowds going up, which is nice."

And the second day? When the alarm went off wasn't he tempted to stay in bed and not put himself out there again? Did anyone try and stop him?

"Not at all. I'm in this for the long haul. And no, no one did. They know me. I may be slow to fall in love but I'm slow to fall out of it. I did recognise a few faces that were there the day before. It's quite touching. Though I don't know if they're there to support me or the novel," he laughs.

"If she isn't interested then I'll move on"

Though he smiles and is good natured throughout, answering almost every question, there's no doubt that Vannes is deadly serious about getting his ex-girlfriend back. On his phone, he shows me photos of their times together.

"Here we are in Naples. We spent five days there. It was our first holiday together. The weather was wonderful. And the food. We went for long walks by the water. It was perfect really."

He shows me others at various times. "Here we are at her friend's birthday. It was the first time I'd met her friends but it went well. They liked me."

He flicks through others photos that he won't allow published. At Thorpe Park, at an Italian restaurant, at Covent Garden, a Chelsea match (Vannes comes from a long line of Chelsea fans and has been a season ticket holder since he was 10). Upon further questions, it turns out the photos were all within the first 18 months. With her striking looks, piercing blue eyes and slim figure that wouldn't be out of place in a pop group or on screen, didn't he worry about losing her?

"I got complacent. I treated her so well in the first year and a half. But Chelsea were doing well, I was getting on great with the guys from work and I got a brand new console and loads of new games. I was like a kid again. I was racking up high scores and having so much fun."

He pauses, and he scrunches his face as he tries answering again. "Not just that. All my closest friends were single and I got carried away with all their energy. I just kept saying yes to all their plans. There was no one else in the picture. She warned me but I thought I was fine. When I got the post-it note I knew I'd messed up."

Ah yes, the post it-note. He shows me the sticky paper, now pretty ruffled, but the writing is certainly still clear. It says simply: "I warned you. Enjoy your gaming. Don't contact me again."

That may seem cold, but Vannes wants to make it clear that though it may sound a brutal way to break up with someone, he had been given repeated warnings. What was his initial reaction when he came home from work to see that note attached to his console?

"If I had to describe it, it was like a part of the sky had fallen in. One day it was there and it was everything. And in one moment, you look up from all the stuff you were distracted by and then it's gone and you wonder how you can ever look at things the same way again."

"It's all about the big gesture"

And so, the questions anyone invested in this story will be asking: Did he tell her what he was doing? Has she been in touch in either of the days since he started?

In short, no and no.

"For a month I'd really tried to get her back. I made every effort I could. She's blocked me now but even if she hadn't I wouldn't. I didn't want to be a pest. This is my last throw of the dice. If she doesn't get back in touch by the time I've finished the novel then I won't contact her again. I just want her to tell me in person either way."

While he hasn't named her, it is surely inevitable that her name will soon come out. Isn't putting the photograph up of someone who might not be comfortable with the spotlight and public attention a very risky move?

He pauses a while before answering. "It's always a possibility. But that's not my intention. And she's very much her own woman. I grew up watching romantic movies. Say Anything with the boombox outside the window. Singing "We've Lost that Loving' Feeling" in Top Gun (it's actually "You've Lost that Loving Feeling"). Building the dream house in The Notebook. We all know how The Graduate ends. It's all about the big gesture."

When I begin to argue that this is real life and not a movie you can switch off, he continues his argument.

"The reason we all love those movies is because we connect with them. They tap into the romance most of us have within us. When the guy, well it can be a girl but it's usually a guy, runs through the airport at the end of the movie, do you root for the guy or the airport security? That's even though the guy has been an idiot for most of the movie. He focused too much on his job, he was going out with the wrong girl, he kept quiet about something when he should have mentioned it at the start.

"He's admitted it and he's prepared to let everyone know because he knows he doesn't want to live without her. And she says yes because he's gone through that journey and they will be better because of it. I truly believe I can make her happier than anybody else.

"And that's all this gesture is. I'm doing everything to get her back. If she isn't interested then that's a real shame. I'll move on and won't contact her again."

It's tempting to wonder if he is leaving anything out. Was he a literary lothario secretly running around behind her back? Did he stalk her at all? Is there anything he is hiding? It does often happen that in relationships there are exterior reasons. Can he confirm he never cheated or even flirted with anyone?

Vannes shakes his head vehemently. "I'm happy to swear on anything you put in front of me that I never cheated or even flirted with any of her friends, or indeed anyone else. I wouldn't be doing this if it was. It would come out and make me look like an a******. Sorry for the language. Feel free to change it to something like a cad or womaniser."

"Love has no numbers"

And his employers? Vannes works as an IT data analyst for a local branch of betting firm

LastGaspWinner.com. Founded five years ago, they cover the sports betting market. Aren't the high profile sports experts worried about the publicity? Aren't they worried about their name getting dragged into this?

"What I do in my personal life isn't remotely to do with work. The guys from my branch met her a few times while we were going out and they all liked her. They all know that if she gave me another chance I'd be the best boyfriend ever. I'm lucky. Because sports are a 24 hour market, at least the way we cover it, I can work some strange hours. I didn't tell them why but I did let them know I would be off mornings so I could do evenings and any weekends and they were fine with that."

Another aspect of the gesture is his voice. Reading out loud for four hours a day would be taxing on anyone, let alone someone who isn't used to it. Surely his voice is cut to ribbons now? It turns out he isn't managing that side of things alone.

"A good friend of mine does radio work. He's given me some great breathing and vocal exercises to help me out, as well as some treatments. And I don't speak much in the evenings. After work I just listen to the radio and then sleep. I'm usually exhausted."

And so, the final question. Does he think it will work? Being a sports man, what odds would he give himself?

"Love has no numbers" he says seriously as he looks back at me. "Some loves aren't easy. It's clear that Heathcliffe and Cathy weren't a conventional love story. But I have hope. I wouldn't be doing this otherwise."

The Tafterton Times wasn't well known or well read. In media terms it was less lobster and more plankton. But today it surely had caught something, and it didn't take long for things to take hold.

Whatever Kurt was thinking, he probably wouldn't have expected the response it got. The Tafterton Times was hardly a big newspaper. In the past he had bought copies as a makeshift umbrella, or else to sit on if he didn't have a blanket when out on a picnic. It contained details about house prices and new shops, as well as local disputes, crime incidents and construction work. It did not have scoops, national stories or any insightful interviews.

So really, Kurt was only expecting something small. He wasn't expecting the journalist to even have it finished for at least another day. But it didn't take him long to realise something was different. Indeed, when he went to get a copy the newsagent was sold out and the newsagent smiled and said he was expecting another delivery within 10 minutes. That journalist must have worked through the night and got some interns to help out. Local printing and the lack of wider delivery helped.

It was a struggle to even get to his near regular spot as people kept coming up to him and asking questions, some even as they were reading the article. As he borrowed a copy from one of the people asking, he sat down to read it and thought it was a balanced article. The journalist had promised there was "no angle and no takedown" and his questions had all been reasonable and fair.

Still, it was still far longer than he had expected. Instead of the small, half page at most story he was expecting, it ran for two pages, with the headline 'Lovestruck Literature Guy Has Novel Idea to get His Girlfriend Back' mentioned on the front page.

Funny, reasoned Kurt. And most of what he had said had made it in. Really, the only stuff left out were his explanations as to why the games were so addictive and how difficult it was to get those high scores. Oh well, it wasn't that important he figured.

Though Kurt took punctuality very seriously these days, he was running late and was already a little flustered. Something that was only added to when he saw the larger number of people waiting, who were all reading the article.

It was far more than he expecting, but still he knew it had to be a good thing. He played poker. Sometimes you don't raise, or re-raise, but go all in. There was no way she could miss all this. She was going to have to get in touch, she couldn't ignore this any longer. How could you say no to anyone who was putting everything on the line to get you back?

Kurt looked out, did a quick scan count and tried to gauge the mood of his audience. It seemed positive enough. Before he started reading, he decided not to bring out the other cards he had from the previous day, or even the one from the opening day. There were more interruptions and more indistinct chatter and a few more camera shots being taken, but he was there to do his reading and was not going to stop.

That was easier said than done though. About half an hour after starting, a local radio DJ shouted out his desires for a radio interview, someone shouted out that Fuchsia had turned up (an effective prank) and there was jostling between the crowd for space at different times. Around two hours or so later, there was an angry confrontation between the vendor and a customer who argued that he hadn't been given the correct change for the new "Brontesaurus Burger". The mood was slightly different, as people who had been there from the very beginning were among those who had come straight over because of the article.

Kurt had remained composed for the most part and was almost finished when a group of females confronted him. There were only four, and were from the nearest university. It was in the next town but they had come especially after hearing about the article. They walked confidently and with purpose towards him.

"We think you're out of order", the group's leader said. She was the youngest and shortest but spoke with clear authority and indignation.

Kurt was completely taken aback and hadn't reacted to that sentence before the 21-year-old carried on with what was a largely prepared speech.

"It's weird, and creepy and possessive, dude. She's not interested. So let it go with all this bullshit. It's stalkery and you're hoping she gives in to public pressure. A woman, any woman, is allowed to say no without needing to feel guilty. Would you like it if she did the same thing to you after you had dumped her?"

Kurt looked at her, her friends who had nodded along at every point and the people around who were listening with great interest as their ideas were being challenged.

"It's not as simple as that. Stalkery is harsh. I've made it clear that if she's uncomfortable with this gesture then I would stop. I'm not going to her flat or her workplace. I'm making an embarrassment of myself for her." He paused for a split second as he looked intently at her. "A question for you."

The girl who had spoken had tried interrupting him a few times but quietened down when he made it clear he was going to ask her a question. She had a confused expression but then nodded.

"Have you ever been in love?" he asked quietly, his voice a bit strained from the long vocal passages.

There was a moment of silence as the girl had not seen the question coming, a sign that Kurt took that he could carry on talking. "You see I have. I'm a sane guy. I know there are people laughing at me. Others like yourself who think I'm a loser, or a stalker as you'd put it. Why? Because I love her. And I was too stupid to realise it earlier. All she has to do and stop it is come and say to my face that she wants it over. Then I'll stop. Until then, I'm taking it as her still thinking it over."

While the main girl was still reflecting his question, one of her friends moved forward and addressed him. "You know it's not as simple as that. You put her photo up, you did the sympathetic interview with a guy not a woman. You could have just done the gesture, but no. You had to stir things up and make her out to be the bad guy."

As quickly as the shots were fired was the response.

"First of all, the picture was an old one so it's not like she can't leave her house without being hassled. Her hair colour is different and the length. And I never gave the journalist her name. And I couldn't care less about whether the interviewer was male or female. He got in touch with me. And in the article I made it very clear I was in the wrong and…"

After a whole life of a low-key existence, Kurt was getting used to defending himself and his actions so would easily have stood his ground and his reasoning. There was only one thing that could have stopped him in his tracks. And it was Fuchsia, or rather Sophia to finally use her real name. And out of nowhere she had appeared.

Kurt looked as though he had seen a ghost. He struggled to stay standing and suddenly felt self-conscious about his appearance. He straightened his already straight tie and combed his hair that was always carefully set.

"Sophia…er.. It's…I know… It's like… er…"

For a man who looked composed not moments ago, it looked like Kurt had forgotten the words to the English language. As he struggled to make a sentence, the crowd slowly started to realise who she was. Some compared her to her photo and could see her hair was different, while others looked at her with a clear pallet. Either way, she was clearly beautiful. That enviable effortless type. She was the nearest thing to perfection Tafterton locals had seen in the flesh.

They may have been sympathetic to his awkward shock, but less so when they started to join the dots and realise how much he had thrown it away.

Finally, Kurt was able to say something. "I was beginning to think you wouldn't come."

Sophia opened her mouth but closed it after a long sigh. But it was clear from her facial expression what she was thinking. And it wasn't good.

"Kurt. It's over. Please end this ghastly freak show."

It's quite something to watch the death of a dream. When hope becomes nothing and all that's left is reality. When sunlight becomes cold, grey skies and the background noise stops and you're left with nothing but your regrets.

There was a video later released which captured his look perfectly, the moment when the light went from his face and he realised he was never going to win. He reacted as though he had been hit in the face, as well as his ribs and legs, as he suddenly swayed a little and looked off balance.

He went to say something, but she shook her head. And it was finally clear to him there was nothing else to say. Sophia pushed through the crowds who suddenly found their voice, put her hands in front of her face to avoid being photographed and hurried off to a waiting car. And with that she was gone.

The ashen-faced Kurt started to pick up his stuff. One or two people went to help. The leader from earlier went up to him. "We knew you were wrong. If you'd listened to us…"

Kurt's initial reaction to this student's comment was rage but by the time his words came out they were different. "You know what? I may be an idiot, quite some idiot, but I'm not cruel. I bid you good day."

And with that he too was gone. He jumped in front of a cab, almost getting himself run over, and then got in. Doubtless breaking the speed limit, the car sped off.

As everyone discussed what was going on, it took more than a few minutes to process everything. It really had all happened so fast. And it was now over. Just like that. The book was still there, as were the placards but now it was just a crowd without a focal point. They soon started to disperse as they made sense of it all, some looking at whatever footage they had captured while others ringing the local newspaper.

And of course, there were all kinds of fallouts and endings.

The Tafterfton Times had sent along a photographer to the event so were able to get plenty of great shots of the action. A house fire had meant the journalist of the story had not been able to make it for a follow up, and a staff shortage had meant they were unable to send anyone else. With people ringing in they were able to get a pretty conclusive set of events and with some video footage able to piece together the dialogue.

And those two stories led to national attention.

While local reaction had been favourable to Kurt, swept aside by the romance of it all, the outside world was not. While a few highlighted good intentions, they argued that it was too possessive and that he had embarrassed her. Most went further. Award-winning columnists with skilled precision and increasing logic argued that the "stunt" was just a form of blackmail and that she didn't owe him an explanation. As an adult, she was allowed to make her judgements and not be guilted into taking him back. And it was hard to argue with that.

But this being a small town with some very entrepreneurial people, they were more interested in the small details. T-shirts of 'Ghastly Freak Show' went on sale. The local sports radio DJ would finish any rants to callers with "I bid you good day". A local musician wrote and performed a song "At least Kurt had a worse day than me" which lasted about a week before it got old. The book and placards had been stolen and were never found.

The journalist of the original story also got further attention. After being criticised for being too lenient with his questioning, he explained on talk shows that the piece was about getting Vannes to explain the logic for his behaviour and get a mindset into this very peculiar man. He said those critical would not find any quotes where he supported his actions, but would instead find a wide array of information and detail that had kickstarted a debate.

And it worked. He looked good on TV and was so comfortable that his profile was raised and he soon started working on a national paper. Not just that. Sophia also got in touch with him. Making it very clear that it was all off the record, she wanted to give her side of things and explained how even in those 18 months, things had been far from perfect. What started off as filling in gaps when she had agreed to meet him, stretched into more conversations about the article, the "stunt" and wider social implications, before it naturally progressed onto other topics and other dates and then a relationship.

Marcus read all the latest developments with interest. He had asked around and tried to find out about Judy but was unsuccessful. Understandably, people weren't keen to volunteer any information. Marcus had to pretend he wanted to give her book back to avoid any further questioning or suspicious looks. But his luck was in. Around a week later he was sitting, having a lukewarm coffee, when Judy walked in carrying a pile of books and a notepad.

This was Marcus's chance. He psyched himself up. This was what he wanted. He went over to say hi, but midway through introducing himself again, a waitress interrupted to ask what she wanted to order. This wasn't like the movies. James Bond never had to worry about this.

Judy remarked on the chances of them running into each other. They talked about the weather, her studies and the time it usually took to get served. But it wasn't anything of any substance. Marcus knew this was small talk and that wasn't good. He asked if she had been reading the articles about Kurt and at the mention of his name, her expression changed and she got defensive and he knew he had no chance.

Marcus got up to go, thinking to himself how he had forgotten to talk about Wuthering Heights. He'd finished it and even read all those stupid essays. Judy gave a polite smile as she went back to her books.

"You really like him, don't you?"

Judy was taken aback by the question. She looked up but Marcus hadn't waited for her answer and had walked out.

The truth was, she did. She had known it almost straight away. She had planned on leaving it a while as things calmed down before contacting him. She figured that he'd be shut off from everyone and it would backfire. But Marcus's clumsy encounter had got her thinking, especially his question at the end. She couldn't hang around any longer.

So, Judy did what she did best. She researched and she pestered. And was well briefed when she went to his offices. When told by the exasperated security guard that he wasn't able to give out employee details she used all manner of tactics to charm him. But all to no avail. As she was thinking up what to do next, one of the guys from the office came out and quietly told her to follow him. Being a bit of an "old softie" he told her of his regular hangout.

And that's where Judy found him. A dark, dingy snooker and pool place filled with illegal smoke and any number of shifty characters. Working her way through the tables she saw Kurt. Unlike everyone else there, he was by himself and was in his own world. The different coloured balls were all over the table but he seemed happy enough as he looked at different angles. When Kurt finally looked up, he saw Judy and smiled.

There's all kinds of ways to finish on, but maybe one of the more sympathetic columnists said it best when quoting Nietzsche. "There is always some madness in love. But there is also always some reason in madness."

Printed in Great Britain
by Amazon

36774167R00026